Usi

When goir
with your child, y
the story first, talking about it
and discussing the pictures,
or start with the sounds pages
at the beginning.

If you start at the front of the book,
read the words and point to the pictures.
Emphasise the **sound** of the letter.

Encourage your child to think
of the other words beginning with
and including the same sound.
The story gives you the opportunity
to point out these sounds.

After the story, slowly go through the
sounds pages at the end.

Always praise and encourage
as you go along. Keep your
reading sessions short and stop
if your child loses interest.

Throughout the series, the order in which the sounds are introduced has been carefully planned to help the important link between reading and writing. This link has proved to be a powerful boost to the development of both skills.

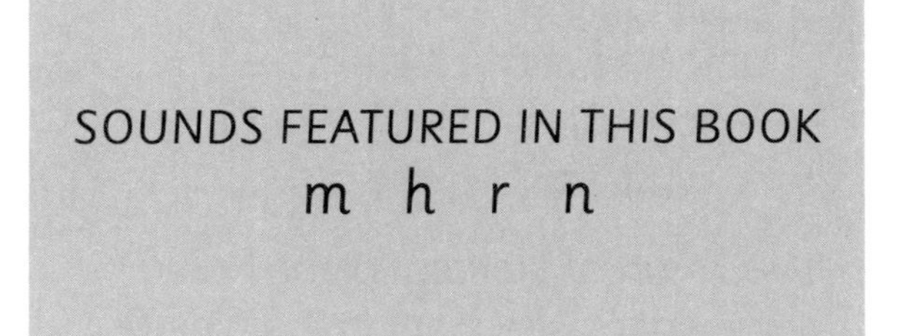

The sounds introduced are repeated and given emphasis in the practice books, where the link between reading and writing is at the root of the activities and games.

Ladybird books are widely available, but in case of difficulty may be ordered by post or telephone from:

Ladybird Books – Cash Sales Department
Littlegate Road Paignton Devon TQ3 3BE
Telephone 0803 554761

A catalogue record for this book is available from the British Library

Published by Ladybird Books Ltd Loughborough Leicestershire UK
Ladybird Books Inc Auburn Maine 04210 USA

Printed in EC

Say the Sounds

Humpty Dumpty and the robots

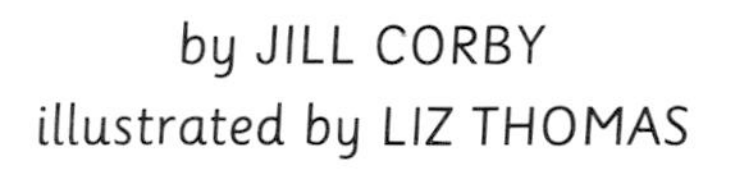

by JILL CORBY
illustrated by LIZ THOMAS

Mm

Say the sound.

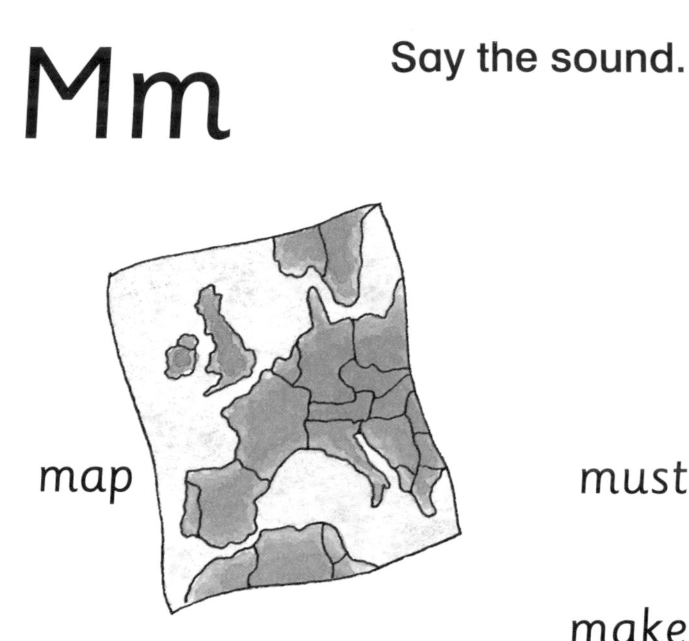

map

must

make

monkey

money

meat

milk

mask

may

mouth

mummy

Monday

march

Hh

Say the sound.

hat

hole

hear

hard

her

head

have

he

horrid

here

has

Rr

Say the sound.

robot

rich

rob

right

run

red

read

rabbit

road

rocket

ring

Nn

Say the sound.

nose

no

nothing

name

night

newspaper

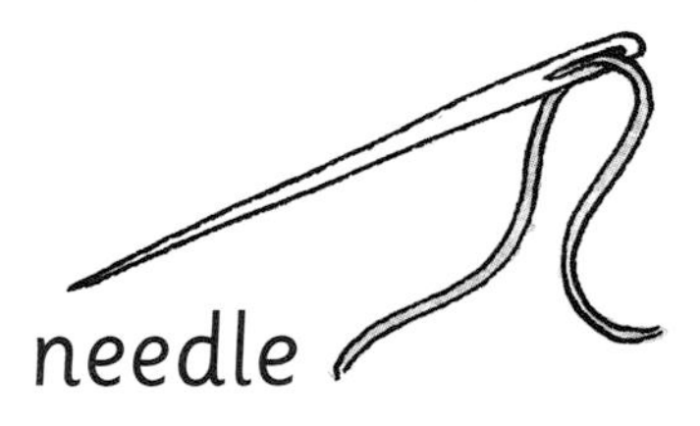
needle

never

not

now

necklace

new

“Mum, please can we make a house?” asked Jenny.

"Can we make it in here please, Mum?" asked Ben.

They have made a nice house.

"You have made a nice house in there," said Mum.

"I have made some tea for Mum," said Dad. "Would you two like your tea in the house?" he asked.

"Here is your tea and two biscuits," Dad said.

"Would you like this biscuit?" Ben asked Jenny.
"Would you like your biscuit now?" Jenny asked Ben.

“This is my bed,” said Jenny.
“And here is my pillow.”
“I have put my bed over there,”
said Ben.
They have made two beds now.

Where are they? They are not in bed now. They have walked down to a big tree.

They saw a man sitting down. It was Mike the Wish Maker.

They walked over to him.
"We know who you are!"
they said.

"Hello, Ben. Hello, Jenny,"
he said.

"Hello, Mike," said Ben and Jenny.
"I'm the man who can make your wishes come true. I'm the Wish Maker!" said Mike, in a big voice.

"Can you make some wishes come true now?" asked Jenny.

Mike made two wishes come true in a very strange voice. He turned Jenny into Rosy Robot and he turned Ben into Ned Robot.

Then Mike the Wish Maker turned and walked off.

Rosy and Ned walked and walked and saw some strange things. They saw some very strange things.

Can you see some strange things?

Then they saw a man sitting
on a wall.
"Who is this?" Rosy asked.
Ned Robot said, "I know who
you are. Humpty Dumpty!"

"Yes, I'm Humpty Dumpty and I'm going to fall off this wall," said Humpty Dumpty, in a high voice.

"You are not going to fall off the wall. You will break," Rosy Robot said.
"You must not break," said Ned. "Stay sitting on the wall."

"I can't stay sitting on this wall. I must fall off now," said Humpty Dumpty. "You can't stop me."

“Yes, we can stop you,” said Ned and Rosy. “You are not going to break.”

Then Rosy saw the King’s Men.

The King's Men are over there.
Look at Humpty Dumpty!
He is going to fall off the wall.

"We must stop him, quickly," said Ned Robot. "Stay sitting on the wall, Humpty Dumpty, and be good," he said.

Humpty Dumpty is sitting on the wall. He will not break now.

"I know he will be good," Ned said to the King's Men.

"The King's Men are going now," Rosy Robot said.

"I can't stay sitting on this wall. I have to fall off and you can't stop me," said Humpty Dumpty. "You know you will break?" Ned asked him.
"Look, I have an idea," said Ned. "Where is your pillow, Rosy?"

"Put your pillow down here by the wall. Put it by me, Rosy."
"Humpty Dumpty can stay on the pillow by the wall. Then he can't fall off," said Rosy.
"That was a good idea, Ned."

"It was a very good idea," said Ned, in a pleased voice.

"Look, here comes Mike the Wish Maker!" said Rosy.

Say the sound.

Read these words.

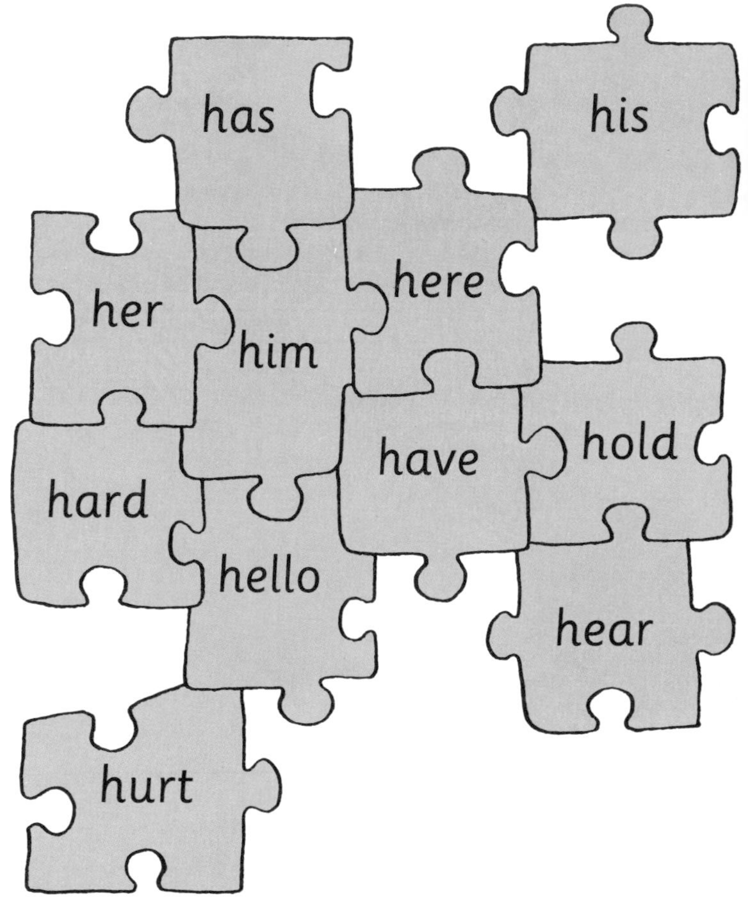

Which things begin with h?

Say the sounds.

m n

Match the sounds to the pictures.

Which things begin with h?

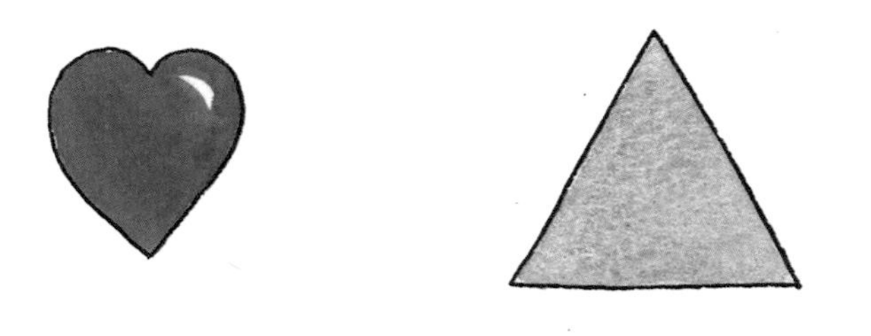

Say the sounds.

Match the sounds to the pictures.

m n

h Which things begin with h?

r Which of these begin with this sound?

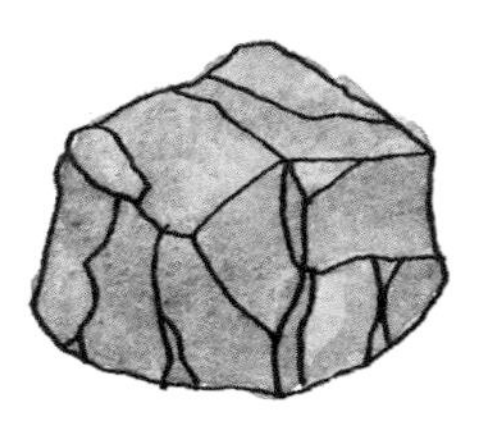

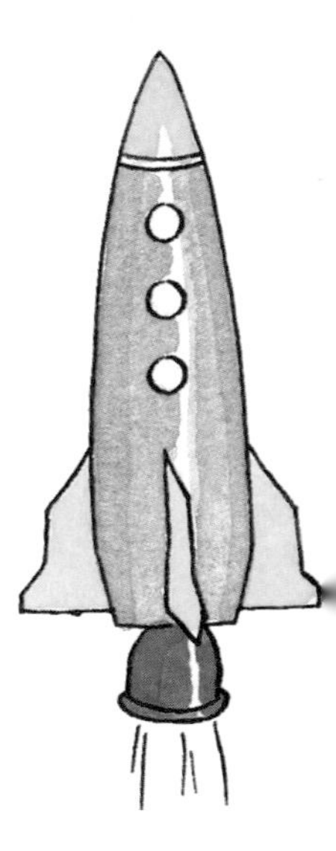

1 2 3 4 5 6 7 8 9 10

New words used in the story

Page Numbers	
12/13	Mum house asked made
14/15	said tea would two biscuit(s)
16/17	my bed(s) pillow put
18/19	walked saw man sitting Mike Wish Maker know who Hello
20/21	I'm wishes true voice strange turned Rosy Robot Ned off

Page Numbers	
22/23	things
24/25	wall Humpty Dumpty fall
26/27	break stay stop me
28/29	King's Men
32/33	by

Words introduced 45

Learn to read with Ladybird

Read with me

A scheme of 16 graded books which uses a look-say approach to introduce beginner readers to the first 300 most frequently used words in the English language (Key Words). Children learn whole words and, with practice and repetition, build up a reading vocabulary.

Support material: Pre-reader, Practice and Play Books, Book and Cassette Packs, Picture Dictionary, Picture Word Cards

Say the Sounds

A phonically based, graded reading scheme of 8 titles. It teaches children the sounds of individual letters and letter combinations, enabling them to feel confident in approaching Key Words.

Support material:
Practice Books, Double Cassette Pack, Flash Cards

Read it yourself

A graded series of 24 books to help children to learn new words in the context of a familiar story. These readers follow on from the pre-reading series, **Read together**, and can be used in conjunction with any Ladybird reading scheme.